# Thomasina and the Trout Tree

Story by Joan Clark
Pictures by Ingeborg Hiscox

Tundra Books 1971

For Gail

©1971, Tundra Books

Published simultaneously
in the United States by
Tundra Books of Northern New York, Plattsburgh, New York
and in Canada by
Tundra Books of Montreal, Montreal 125, Quebec

Designed by Rolf Harder, Design Collaborative
Printed in Canada

Thomasina lived just outside the city, and she often longed for the excitement of downtown. She liked to take a bus to the center of the city. Here everything began or ended, depending on whether she was coming or going.

Today it was a beginning. Thomasina was going to look for the Trout Tree. She was not sure where the Trout Tree was, or even *what* it was. She knew it was a work of art—but what kind of art?

She squeezed two cheese and cherry sandwiches into her back pocket, tickets into her front pocket, and went out on the street to wait for a bus. When it came she got on and passed miles of rectangular houses, round schools and triangular churches. They looked like big kindergarten blocks stacked higher and closer together towards downtown. There, blue sky cut around tall walls of cement and glass like pieces of a jigsaw puzzle.

When she stepped off the bus, the doors hissed at her. Tires squealed when a traffic light turned red. Horns honked. Motors roared. Thomasina watched the bright colors streak by and wondered where in all this sight and sound she would find the Trout Tree. Across the street was a park. That would be a good place to look.

She opened the iron gates. Trees, flowers and shrubs were a living wall of green between her and the man-made part of downtown. She wandered along the paths. Old people sat on shaded benches, their faces carved like statues. Pigeons with marble feathers scattered at her feet. A popsicle man slowly peddled by with an orange-red parrot on his shoulder. Everything was quiet and easy like a slow-motion movie.

Until she reached the pond in the middle of the park.

Here a loud smacking splash broke the hush. Thomasina went to the edge of the water. Right beside a sign that said *no swimming,* a red-haired man with a bushy beard was throwing himself around in the water. He splashed and spluttered away for a few minutes, then ran out of the water, up the bank and jumped into an old bathtub. The tub was filled with purple and black paint.

Thomasina stepped behind a shrub to watch. The wild-looking man rubbed the paint all over himself. Now and then he shouted to a white goat who was tied to a tree nearby.

''It won't be long, Maurice. Have patience, dear one.''

The goat stared in Thomasina's direction.

''There, just a bit more on my back and I'm away.''

When he was completely covered with paint, the man got out of the tub, and spread a piece of paper as big as a carpet on the grass. He then got down on it and rolled back and forth, rubbing the paint off his body. When he had filled in all of the white spots on the paper, he stood up to admire his work.

''Isn't that lovely? Purple and black have such mood. It might be one of my best paintings this week.''

He pulled the wet paper toward the goat. ''Here, dear one. Eat, while it's ripe.''

The goat began to munch the paper. He ate without stopping, ripping off large shreds, until half the painting was gone. Then unexpectedly, his legs buckled under him and he fell on the uneaten part. His feet twitched. He was breathing heavily.

"Oh, my poor Maurice, dear one. What have I done? What have I done?"

The red-haired man got down on his knees and began to rock back and forth.

Thomasina could stand by and watch no longer. She stepped out of her hiding place.

"What's the big idea, feeding paper to a goat?" she said angrily.

The man looked up, startled. "Paper? Paper? Who's feeding him paper?"

"You are."

He stood up and waved his hands around. "That is *not* paper. It is a painting. It *was* paper until I, the Great Vincent," he was shouting now, "changed it into a masterpiece."

"But why," asked Thomasina, "feed it to him?"

"Simple. Simple. Because he has a taste for modern art!"

Maurice started to moan.

The Great Vincent took the goat's head in his lap. "There, there, dear one. You'll soon be better."

But Maurice seemed to be getting worse. His legs jerked. His mouth foamed.

The Great Vincent grabbed Thomasina's hand and yelled: *"Do something!"*

"Do something?" echoed Thomasina." What can I do?"

"Something! Anything! Save him! Please."

She was at a loss. Should she go for a doctor? Run to the drug store? Then she had an idea.

"Do you usually give him such dark paintings?"

The Great Vincent did not hear her. He was sobbing as loud as Maurice was moaning.

She put her mouth to his ear, *"Do you usually feed him such dark paintings?"*

"No. They are usually bright. That's it! He needs a bright painting to cure the dark one. I knew the dark one was powerful. You do it. Roll him a light bright painting."

"Me?" cried Thomasina. "But I've never painted anything except a birdhouse."

"That doesn't matter. Just take a quick dip in the pond. Squeeze some paints into the tub and jump in. When you are covered with lightness and brightness, have a roll on the paper."

"Oh, no. I couldn't," Thomasina said.

The goat moaned louder and the Great Vincent cried harder. It was no time to think of herself. She dumped the dark paint out, and squeezed tubes of yellow, pink and green into the tub. Then she added a dash of orange. As she took her shoes off to step in, the Great Vincent yelled: "Water! Water! You've got to get wet."

Ducks scattered as she ran into the pond. Mud oozed up between her toes. She splashed herself quickly, then ran back and stepped into the tub. Now paint oozed up between her toes.

She would have changed her mind about the whole thing, but the Great Vincent kept calling, "Atta girl! Atta girl!"

She sat down slowly. The cold clammy paint clung to her jeans. Holding her hair up on her head with one hand, she dabbed paint on with the other until she was wearing a sample of each color. Then she got out of the tub and lay down on a piece of paper.

The Great Vincent yelled, "Roll! Roll!"

She rolled over once, twice, back and forth like a rolling pin. The green trees, the red-orange flowers, the blue sky, all ran together into a kaleidoscope of color. This was fun. She didn't want to stop, but again, she heard the voice in her ear, *"That's enough! Maurice is sinking fast!"*

Thomasina got up and before she had a chance to admire her painting, the Great Vincent jerked it toward the goat. He stuffed a corner into Maurice's mouth. The goat swallowed it. The Great Vincent fed him more. In a short time Maurice had eaten the whole painting.

"That was a work of art," said the Great Vincent approvingly.

"It was?" Thomasina wished more than ever she had taken a good look at her painting before Maurice ate it.

The Great Vincent began sorting out his tubes of paint.

"Why, you painter of birdhouses," he said, accusingly. "You've used all of my light bright paints. I'll have to get more."

Without saying so much as a "thank you" or a "goodbye", he dashed down the path, his red hair streaming, and out onto the street.

"He certainly is unpredictable, isn't he?" Thomasina said to Maurice.

Maurice yawned. He could hardly keep his eyes open.

Thomasina patted the white tuft on his head. "You had better get some rest while you can. I hope you get nothing but bright paintings from now on, though I won't be rolling them for you."

And leaving him to sleep, she strode down the path through the shrubbery. She was rounding a bend when something— a someone on hands and knees—streaked across the path, knocking her backwards so that she fell into a juniper bush. The someone turned out to be a long thin policeman, all angles and bones, who was crawling toward a shiny object.

He picked it up.

"By Jove," he exclaimed, "it's just what I need."

He got up, brushed the dirt off his uniform, which had shrunk from being washed too many times, straightened his cap and was about to leave when Thomasina spoke up. Policeman or not, she was annoyed.

"Do you usually trip people by crawling across the path?"

He turned around.

"Oh, I'm frightfully sorry," he said, so nicely that she was sorry she had said anything. "Be a sport and allow me to help you out of that bush." He held out a long arm. Thomasina took his hand and pulled herself up.

"I get carried away with my hobby," the policeman explained.

"Is your hobby picking up things?"

"That's only part of it, a very small part. It's the putting-together of things that I pick up that's important. I fancy myself a bit of an artist."

Thomasina was curious. "What kind of artist?"

"Come, see." He led the way to a large elm tree. It held a bulletin board with the words *Lost and Found* printed neatly across the top. Tacked to the board were a lace glove, shoelaces, a brocade case for glasses, a small black purse, a pearl brooch, a wallet, two pencils, a watch chain and a velvet hair band. The policeman put the shiny object in the middle of the board. It was a rhinestone earring.

"There! That sets it off, don't you think? What it needed was sparkle." He fussed with the objects, moving them about until he was satisfied.

"I call this *City Park 609*," he said proudly.

"But I thought it was *Lost and Found*."

"It is. It's that *and* it's art. It's useful *and* beautiful. And it changes all the time. As people come along and claim their lost things, I find other things to put up. I'm always adding or subtracting. A new work of art every day! Yesterday it was *City Park 608*."

"And tomorrow it will be *City Park 610?*" asked Thomasina.

"Exactly. You understand perfectly. Say, I'm glad I ran you down." Then embarrassed at his own words, he said: "I usually nip into the police station for a spot of tea about this time. You look like you could use some, and a washing up."

Thomasina had forgotten she was still wearing some of the Great Vincent's light bright paint.

The police station turned out to be a small brick cottage behind the elm tree. It had two doors. One led to the gardener's tool shed and the other to a cozy room with a table and chairs, a desk piled halfway to the ceiling with books and papers, and a small stove.

The policeman pointed to a sink. "You can wash up over there while I make some tea."

In a few minutes Thomasina's skin was pink and shining. She sat down at the table and took out the cheese and cherry sandwiches. She offered one to the policeman, then took a sip out of the cup in front of her. One gulp told her it was only hot water. He had forgotten to add the tea. She looked in his cup. It too was filled with hot water but he didn't seem to notice.

"Jolly good sandwiches. Are you on your way somewhere, or just spending the day in the park?"

"I'm going to see the Trout Tree—if I can find it."

"It's probably on the other side of the Neon Jungle. Where, I couldn't say, but the Lady-in-Waiting lives in the jungle and she might know."

Up to now Thomasina had thought policemen were good at giving directions. This one was different. Suddenly a sharp-faced woman wearing one rhinestone earring stuck her head in the door.

"Have you seen my earring?"

The policeman stood up, then marched forward like a wind-up toy. "Right this way, madam."

At the door he turned to Thomasina. "Help yourself to more tea."

As soon as he was gone, she ran out the door. The thought of drinking more hot water was not one she liked. Besides, she had to find the Trout Tree. She opened the iron gates, stepped onto the hot pavement and was carried along by the crowds.

In the park she had forgotten about time. Now a huge clock with red hands and orange numbers kept blinking each second. Lights flashed at her from all directions. Theater marquees were blobs of moving white lights. Store fronts beat out color like the wings of tropical birds. Giant billboards splashed the sky with colors. This must be the Neon Jungle.

As colors whirled around her, dump trucks clattered past, construction hammers clanged and an electric drill whined. Everyone was in a hurry, including Thomasina. She had gone four blocks when she saw a sign in a dingy shop window. Wobbly black letters read: *Yoga Lessons by the Lady-in-Waiting.* Beside the sign, a woman stood on her head. She wore black leotards, and her hair flowed around her like black liquid. No one on the street paid any attention, except Thomasina. The woman could have been a mannequin, except that mannequins are usually right-side-up.

A bell over the door tinkled as Thomasina entered the shop. There was nothing in the shop except some large chunks of stone, some unfinished sculptures and a table with hammers and chisels.

''Have you come for lessons?'' the woman called. Her voice was tinkly like the bell over the door.

''I've come to see the Trout Tree.''

''Can you stand on your head?''

''A little bit.''

''Do join me. It's good for your health and absolutely the best way to talk.''

Thomasina stood on her head in the window.

Because she and the Lady-in-Waiting were on their heads and everyone on the other side of the glass was not, the conversation was very private.

"I always thought a Lady-in-Waiting worked for queens and princesses," Thomasina said.

The Lady-in-Waiting laughed. "Oh, I'm not that sort of Lady-in-Waiting. I'm a lady and I'm waiting."

"What are you waiting for?"

"I don't know exactly."

"How can you wait for something if you don't know what it is?"

The Lady-in-Waiting sighed. "It isn't easy. But I'm used to it. To pass the time I give yoga lessons and make sculptures. When I start a sculpture, I feel this time I will make a great work of art. But after a while my head hurts and I have to stand on it again."

"Why don't you sculpt standing on your head?" Thomasina suggested.

The Lady-in-Waiting thought about this. "I might try that some day. I've been working on that tree over there ever so long but I just can't finish it."

"Why not?" asked Thomasina.

"Because I can never finish anything," she sighed again. "I can't bear to. There's something so final about coming to the end."

Thomasina looked at a tall chunk of marble in the corner.
It was upside down, but she could see the outline of a tree.

"Is that the Trout Tree?" she asked.

"I really couldn't say," said the Lady-in-Waiting. "Until it's
finished, it could be anything."

Thomasina looked at it again and decided it was not the Trout
Tree. She was sure the real thing would be finished.

"*My* head is beginning to hurt," Thomasina said. "I think I'll
be going."

"Pardon me if I don't see you to the door, "said the Lady-in-
Waiting," but I must catch up on my waiting."

And Thomasina left the Lady-in-Waiting still standing on her
head.

As Thomasina stepped out on the street, she was caught again in the fast-moving stream of people. She travelled block after block before the crowd thinned out and she slowed down. She stopped to look in the window of a Chinese tea shop. A mobile of large paper fish floated in the air. The wires holding the fish were fastened to a branch tacked up on the wall. An electric fan kept the fish moving.

The fish were lime green, ice blue, canary yellow, Halloween orange and magenta.

For a moment she thought this might be the Trout Tree but she quickly changed her mind. The fish looked more like whales than trout.

She continued along the sidewalk. Rays of the sun came through slits between the skyscrapers. Already it was mid-afternoon and she still hadn't found the Trout Tree.

Across the street a wooden fence enclosed a corner lot. On it were neat red letters: *Mike's Junkyard.* Sitting on a stool at the entrance was a little man wearing goggles.

Thomasina crossed over and looked through the gate. Behind the fence was the cleanest junkyard she had ever seen. Wrecked cars were neatly lined up in rows. Odd pieces of rusted metal were stacked in brightly painted bins.

She watched the little man. He was holding a piece of metal over a welding torch, carefully turning it. The yellow-blue flame bent the metal into a large spoon without a handle. He turned off the torch, took off his goggles and held the metal up to Thomasina.

"Now, what do you think of that?" he said in a lilting voice that was like a handful of notes thrown into her ear. "You wouldn't think something like this could be made out of scrap, now would you?"

"But what use is it? It has no handle."

"Why would I want to put a handle on it?"

"I thought it was a spoon," said Thomasina.

The little man laughed so hard he nearly fell off his stool.

"Well, what is it then?" said Thomasina in a loud voice.

The little man stood up, but he was so short, he barely came up to her shoulder. With his large ears, furry eyebrows and emerald-green eyes he looked like an Irish leprechaun. He bent close to her and spoke in a whisper. "It's a fish for my tree."

Thomasina's heart made an excited leap.

"Is it for the Trout Tree?" she whispered back.

"The Trout Tree?" His eyes crinkled at the corners. "Why would you be wanting to see such a thing?"

"Because it's a work of art."

"Is it now? Then I, Mike O'Flanagan, have such a work of art."

"You have? How wonderful! I've been looking for it all day."

Mike grinned and whispered. "I don't have it right here. I keep it in a special place—under lock and key. You do want to see it?"

"Oh, yes. Please!"

Mike took a key chain from his pocket and removed three keys.

"This way," he whispered.

He went down a row of cars and stopped in front of a red convertible. He took one of the three keys, opened the door, climbed into the car and beckoned her to follow. When they were both inside, he led the way out the opposite door.
The car had been stripped of its seats, so passing through it was easy. Mike locked the car door carefully after them.
Next he unlocked and relocked a green car before and after they climbed in and out of that. Then he did the same thing with a yellow one.

This was too much for Thomasina. "Why," she asked, "do you go *through* cars when it is easier to walk *around* them?"

Mike winked at her. "I don't want just anybody going through here, now do I?"

"No, of course not," said Thomasina, feeling very special.

Mike now led the way to a square black Ford set on concrete slabs. Two steps went up to the door. Through the window, Thomasina could see a bed, table and chairs, all shining clean.

"This is my home," Mike said proudly. Then he pointed even more proudly to something bigger than the car, "and this is my work of art."

Thomasina looked. Near the car a metal tree stood in a round metal pond. Metal fish hung from the branches. Even the fish swimming beneath the water's surface looked metallic. Everywhere metal reflected the sun.

"It's beautiful," said Thomasina. "Did you make it yourself?"

"That I did," Mike said. "The trunk and the branches are from pipes. I turned the junkyard scraps into a work of art. It took me a long time but that's the way I live. Art is living, don't you think?"

But Thomasina didn't answer. She was staring at something green covering two fish at the bottom of the tree.

"This tree has something extra special about it," Mike went on. "Watch!" He bent over and turned a knob on the metal trunk.

Water sprayed from the branches and fell like fine rain on the pond beneath. As it fell, the metal fish jingled against one another, making thin watery music.

"It's a fountain!" Thomasina laughed, delighted. "Oh, it *is* a work of art!"

Then she noticed that the two fish with green on them weren't jingling. She tried to ignore them, but they spoiled the tree.

"What are those green things hanging in the tree?" she asked.

Mike's eyes twinkled with pride. "They're my socks. These metal fish make dandy sock stretchers. And that's not all. On wash day I hang my soiled clothes on the branches and turn on the fountain. I can't use soap because I wouldn't want to kill the fish. Still, the clothes come clean enough for me. Then I turn off the water and they dry in the sun."

Thomasina stared at him in horror. ''You mean you use a work of art for a washing machine?''

Mike looked ashamed. ''Only on Mondays,'' he said, in a small voice. ''And in between for sock stretching.''

But Thomasina was not satisfied.

''Are those trout in the water?'' she asked, very suspicious now.

''No, they're carp,'' admitted Mike.

So this wasn't the Trout Tree after all. It was a work of art, certainly. But it wasn't the one she had been looking for all day. It was then she realized that there was no such thing as the Trout Tree. It was simply an idea. But she would change that. She would make her own Trout Tree.

''I'll be fishing out a carp for my supper tonight,'' Mike said. ''Would you like to stay and I'll fish out two?''

''No, thank you, Mike. I must go home. I've got something special to do.''

Mike insisted she leave by way of the red, green and yellow cars, but she was still on time to catch the express bus home.

All the way back she thought of different ways of making her own Trout Tree.

Should she twist coat hangers into a tree, put it in a wading pool and add real trout?

Should she spray a branch purple and hang foil fish from it?
Should she…?

The possibilities were endless.